Sunny the Yellow Fairy

To the fairies at the
bottom of my garden

Special thanks to
Sue Bentley

ISBN 0-439-69195-8

17 16 15   12/0

Printed in the U.S.A.

First Scholastic printing, November 2004

Sunny the Yellow Fairy

by Daisy Meadows
illustrated by Georgie Ripper

SCHOLASTIC INC.

New York Toronto London Auckland Sydney
Mexico City New Delhi Hong Kong Buenos Aires

Jack Frost's Ice Castle

Tom Goodfellow's House

Merry-go-round

Willow Tree

Mrs. Merry's Cottage

Stream

Field

Mermaid Cottage

Town

Harbor

Dolphin Cottage

Cold winds blow and thick ice forms,
I conjure up this fairy storm.
To seven corners of the mortal world
the Rainbow Fairies will be hurled!

I curse every part of Fairyland,
with a frosty wave of my icy hand.
For now and always, from this fateful day,
Fairyland will be cold and gray!

Ruby and Amber have been rescued.
Now it's time to search for
Sunny the **Yellow Fairy**

Contents

A Very Fierce Bee

"Over here, Kirsty!" called Rachel Walker. Kirsty ran down one of the emerald-green fields that covered this part of Rainspell Island. Buttercups and daisies dotted the grass.

"Don't go too far!" Kirsty's mom called. She and Kirsty's dad were climbing over a fence at the top of the field.

Kirsty caught up with her friend.

"What have you found, Rachel? Is it another Rainbow Fairy?" she asked hopefully.

"I don't know." Rachel was standing on the bank of a rippling stream. "I thought I heard something."

Kirsty's face lit up. "Maybe there's a fairy in the stream?"

Rachel nodded. She knelt down on the soft grass and put her ear close to the water.

Kirsty crouched down, too, and listened really hard.

The sun glittered on the water as it splashed over big, shiny pebbles. Tiny rainbows flashed and sparkled — red, orange, yellow, green, blue, indigo, and violet.

And then they heard a tiny bubbling voice. "Follow me. . . ." it gurgled. "Follow me. . . ."

"Oh!" Rachel gasped. "Did you hear that?"

"Yes," said Kirsty, her eyes wide. "It must be a *magic* stream!"

Rachel felt her heart beat fast.

"Maybe the stream will lead us to the Yellow Fairy," she said.

Rachel and Kirsty had a special secret. They had promised the King and Queen of Fairyland they would find the lost Rainbow Fairies. Jack Frost's spell had hidden the Rainbow Fairies on Rainspell Island. Fairyland would be cold and gray until all seven fairies had been found and returned to their home.

Silver fish darted in and out of the bright green weeds at the bottom of the stream. "Follow us, follow us. . . ." they whispered in tinkling voices.

Rachel and Kirsty smiled at each other. Titania, the Fairy Queen, had said that the magic would find them!

Kirsty's parents had stopped to admire the stream, too. "Which way now?" asked Mr. Tate. "You two seem to know where you're going."

"Let's go this way," Kirsty said, pointing along the bank.

A brilliant blue kingfisher flew up from its perch on a twig. Butterflies as bright as jewels fluttered among the reeds.

"Everything on Rainspell Island is so beautiful," said Kirsty's mom. "I'm glad we still have five days of vacation left!"

Yes, Rachel thought, *and five Rainbow Fairies still to find: Sunny, Fern, Sky, Inky — and Heather!*

Ruby the Red Fairy and Amber the Orange Fairy were already safe in the pot-at-the-end-of-the-rainbow.

The girls ran on ahead of Mr. and Mrs. Tate. As they followed the bubbling stream, the sun went behind a big, dark cloud.

A chilly breeze ruffled Kirsty's hair. She
saw that some of the leaves on the trees
were turning brown,
even though it
wasn't autumn.
"It looks like
Jack Frost's
goblins are still
around," she
warned Rachel.

"I know." Rachel
shivered. "Horrible
things! They'll do
anything to stop the Rainbow
Fairies from getting back to
Fairyland."

The two friends stared anxiously up
at the sky. But then the sun came out
again. They smiled with relief.

The stream ran through a meadow covered with green clover. A herd of black-and-white cows was grazing at the water's edge. They looked up with their huge, brown eyes.

"Aren't they lovely?" Kirsty said.

Suddenly, the cows tossed their heads and ran off toward the other end of the field.

Rachel and Kirsty looked at each other in surprise. What was going on?

There was a loud buzzing noise.

A small angry shape came whizzing
through the air, straight toward them!
Rachel almost jumped
out of her skin. "It's
a bee!" She gasped.
"Run!" Kirsty cried.
The cows had
the right idea!
Rachel tore through the
meadow with Kirsty beside
her, their feet pounding the grass.
"Keep running, girls," called Mr. Tate,
catching up with them. "That bee
seems to be following us!"

Rachel glanced
back. The bee was
huge, bigger than
any bee she'd
ever seen.

"In here, quick!" Mrs. Tate called from the side of the field. She pulled open a wooden gate.

They all ran through it, then stopped to catch their breath.

"I wonder who lives here." Kirsty panted. They were in a beautiful yard. A path led up to a thatched cottage with yellow roses around the door.

Just then, a very strange creature came out from behind some trees. It looked like an alien from outer space!

"Oh!" Rachel and Kirsty gasped.

The creature lifted its gloved hands and removed its white helmet to reveal . . . an older woman! She smiled at them. "Sorry if I startled you," she said. "I do look a bit strange in my beekeeper's suit."

Rachel sighed in relief. It wasn't a space alien after all!

"I'm Mrs. Merry," the old lady went on.

"Hello," Rachel said. "I'm Rachel. This is my friend Kirsty."

"And this is my mom and dad," Kirsty added.

Mr. and Mrs. Tate greeted Mrs. Merry. Then Mr. Tate ducked as the huge bee zoomed past his ear. "Watch out!" he said.

"Oh, it's that hiveless queen again," said Mrs. Merry. She flapped her hand at the bee. "Go on, shoo!" Rachel watched it swoop over a low hedge and disappear.

"Why did the bee chase us?" Kirsty
asked.

"I don't think she was chasing you,
my dear," said Mrs. Merry. "She was
just heading this way because she's
looking for a hive of her own. But all
of my hives already have queens."

"Well, thank goodness she's gone
now!" said Mrs. Tate.

"Since you're here, would you like to
try some of my honey?" Mrs. Merry
asked. Her blue eyes sparkled merrily.

"Oh, yes, please," said Rachel.

The others nodded, and
they followed Mrs. Merry
across the lawn to a table
covered with rows
of jars.

Each jar was filled with rich golden honey. Dappled sunlight danced over the jars, making the honey glow.

"Here you are," said Mrs. Merry, spooning some honey onto a pretty yellow plate.

"Thank you," Rachel said politely. She dipped her finger into the little pool of honey and popped it into her mouth. The honey was the most delicious she had ever tasted — sweet and smooth.

Then she felt it ⌐⌐⌐⌐⌐⌐⌐⌐⌐
tongue. She looked ac⌐⌐⌐
tastes all fizzy!" she whispe⌐
    Kirsty dipped her finger into ⌐
honey, too. "And look!" she said.
    Rachel saw that the honey was
sparkling with a thousand tiny, gold
lights. She grabbed Kirsty's arm. "Do
you think this means —"
    "Yes," said Kirsty. Her eyes were
shining. "Another Rainbow Fairy must
be nearby!"

The Magic Hive

"We have to find out where this honey came from!" Rachel said excitedly.

"Yes," Kirsty agreed. "Mom? Can we stay here a bit longer, please?"

"As long as it's OK with Mrs. Merry," Kirsty's mom replied.

Mrs. Merry beamed. "Of course they can stay," she said kindly.

Mr. and Mrs. Tate decided to continue their walk. "Make sure you come back to Dolphin Cottage by lunchtime," Kirsty's mom said.

"We will," Kirsty promised.

"Come along then, girls." Mrs. Merry set off across the smooth, green lawn.

Rachel and Kirsty followed her down the yard to some old and twisted apple trees. Six wooden hives stood underneath.

Kirsty stared at the row of hives.

"Which one did the honey we tasted come from?" she asked.

Mrs. Merry looked pleased. "Did you enjoy it? The honey from that hive tastes especially good at the moment."

Rachel and Kirsty grinned at each other.

"I think we might know why," Rachel whispered to Kirsty.

"Yes," Kirsty agreed. "It could be fairy honey!"

"That's the one," Mrs. Merry said proudly, pointing to the very back of the yard. One hive stood there all alone, beneath the biggest apple tree.

As they drew nearer to the hive,
a sleepy buzzing sound drifted
up into the air.
"The bees in this hive
are very peaceful
nowadays," said
Mrs. Merry.
"I've never known
them to be so happy."

"Can we get a bit closer?" Rachel
asked eagerly. She couldn't wait to find
out if the hive held a magical secret!

Mrs. Merry looked thoughtful. "I think
it's safe, with the bees so quiet," she
decided. "But you had better wear a
hood like mine, just in case."

She went into a nearby shed and
brought out two beekeepers' hoods.
"Here you are."

Rachel and Kirsty pulled the hoods over their heads. It was a bit dark and stuffy inside but they could see out of the fine netting.

They moved closer to the hive. The soft buzzing sounded almost like music.

"We need to open it and take a look," Kirsty whispered to Rachel.

Rachel nodded.

But they couldn't start searching for
the Yellow Fairy with Mrs. Merry there.
Ruby had warned them that no grown-
ups should see the fairies.

Suddenly, Kirsty had an idea. "Mrs.
Merry, could I have a drink of water,
please?" she asked.

"Of course you can, dear," Mrs.
Merry said. She went off toward the
cottage.

The girls waited until Mrs. Merry
disappeared inside.

"Quick!" Kirsty spun around. "Let's
open the hive."

Rachel grasped one end of the lid.
Kirsty took hold of the other end. They
pulled hard, and it slowly came loose
with a squeaky sound. Strings of golden
honey stretched down from the lid.

"Watch out. It's very sticky," Rachel said.

The girls bent down and laid the heavy wooden top carefully on the ground. Kirsty wiped her fingers on the grass.

"Look!" Rachel whispered as she stood up.

Kirsty turned to see, and gasped.

A shower of sparkling gold dust shot up out of the hive. It hung in a soft cloud, shimmering and dancing in the sunlight. Fairy dust!

Rachel leaned over and peered down into the hive. A tiny girl was sitting cross-legged on a piece of honeycomb, in the middle of a golden sea of honey.

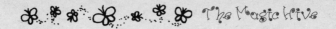

A bee lay with its head in her lap while she combed its silky hair. Several other bees were waiting their turn, buzzing gently.

"Oh, Kirsty," Rachel whispered. "We've found another Rainbow Fairy!"

Bee Friends

Rachel and Kirsty took off their hoods and stared down into the hive in delight.

The fairy had bright yellow hair. She wore a necklace of golden raindrops around her neck and sparkly golden bracelets on both wrists. Her bright yellow T-shirt and shorts were the color of buttercups. Her delicate

wings glistened with a thousand shimmering rainbows.

"Oh, thank you for finding me!" the
fairy said in a tinkling voice. "I'm
Sunny the Yellow Fairy."

"I'm Rachel,"
said Rachel.
"And I'm Kirsty,"
said Kirsty.
"We've met two
of your sisters
already — Ruby
and Amber."
Sunny beamed
happily.
"You've found
Ruby and Amber?"
She stood up, gently
pushing the bee away.

"Yes. They're safe in the pot-at-the-end-of-the-rainbow," Rachel said.

Sunny clapped her tiny hands. "I can't *wait* to see them again." Suddenly, she looked worried. "Have you seen any of Jack Frost's goblins near here?" she asked.

"No, not here," Kirsty said. "But there were some by the pot yesterday."

"We hid in a bush until they went away," Rachel explained.

"Goblins are scary," Sunny said in a trembling voice. "I've been safe from them here in the hive, with my friends the bees." Rachel felt very sorry for Sunny. "It's all right. King Oberon sent one of his frog footmen to look after you and your sisters." Sunny cheered up. "I've been really worried about finding my sisters. Jack Frost's magic is so cold and strong." "It won't be long now," Kristy said. "We are going to find Fern, Sky, Inky, and Heather, too, aren't we, Rachel?" "Yes. We promised," Rachel agreed.

"Oh, thank you!" Sunny said. She threw out her arms and gave a shake of her sparkling wings.

Fairy dust rose into the air and drifted down around Rachel and Kirsty. Where it landed, bright yellow butterflies appeared, with tiny fluttering wings.

A large bee crawled from one of the waxy openings in the honeycomb next to Sunny.

"This is my best friend, Queenie," said Sunny. She put her arms around the bee's neck and kissed the top of her furry head.

Queenie buzzed softly.

"She says hello," said Sunny.

"Hello, Queenie," Kirsty and Rachel said together.

Sunny picked up her tiny comb and began to comb Queenie's shiny hair. Another bee buzzed angrily.

"Don't worry, Petal, I'll comb your hair next," Sunny said.

Rachel and Kirsty looked at each other in dismay.

"What if Sunny wants to stay with Queenie and the other bees?" Kirsty whispered.

"Sunny, you have to come with us!" Rachel burst out. "Or Fairyland will never get its colors back! It will take all of the Rainbow sisters to undo Jack Frost's spell."

Forgetful Fairy

"Yes, of course! We have to break Jack Frost's spell!" Sunny cried. She jumped to her feet and picked up her wand.

Suddenly, an icy wind sprang up. Something crunched under Kirsty's feet. The grass was covered with frost!

Rachel shivered as something soft and cold brushed against her cheek.

A snowflake in summer? "What's happening?" she cried.

"Jack Frost's goblins must be near," Kirsty said worriedly.

Sunny's tiny teeth chattered with cold. "Oh, no! If they find me, they will stop me from getting back to Fairyland!"

Kirsty looked at Rachel in alarm. "Quick, we have to go!"

Rachel leaned down and lifted the fairy out of the hive.

Sunny's golden hair dripped with honey.

"Oh, dear, you're really sticky," Rachel said.

Just then, Kirsty spotted Mrs. Merry coming out of her cottage.

"I'd forgotten about asking for a drink," Kirsty said. "What are we going to do?"

Rachel thought for a moment, then popped the fairy into the pocket of her shorts.

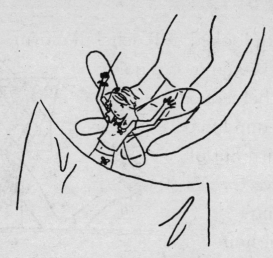

Sunny gave a cry of dismay. "Hey! It's dark in here!" she complained.

"Sorry," Rachel whispered. "I'll get you out again in a minute."

Suddenly, Kirsty noticed the open hive. "We have to put the top back on!" she said.

She bent down and grasped the lid. Rachel helped lift it and they quickly put it back, just as Mrs. Merry came through the trees.

"Here's your drink, dear," said Mrs. Merry, holding out a glass to Kirsty. She had taken off her strange suit, and in her other hand she was carrying a shopping basket.

"Thank you very much," Kirsty said, taking the glass.

"Now, you girls stay as long as you like," said Mrs. Merry. "I've just remembered I must go and buy some fish for my cat."

Rachel watched Mrs. Merry go toward the garden gate. Then she slipped her hand into her pocket.

"You can come out now," she said to Sunny, lifting her out.

The fairy was covered with gray fluff from Rachel's pocket. "Achoo!" She sneezed. She brushed angrily at the bits of sticky fluff clinging to her wings. "I'm all clogged up!" she wailed. "I won't be able to fly."

"We need to clean you up," Rachel said. "But we'll have to be quick, in case the goblins find us."

Kirsty looked around and spotted a stone birdbath filled with clear water. "Over there." She pointed.

"Just what we need," Rachel agreed. She carried Sunny over to the birdbath.

Sunny fluttered onto the edge of the bath, put down her wand, and dived in.

Splash!

The water fizzed and turned bright yellow. Lemony-smelling drops shot everywhere.

Sunny swam two circles, then she was sparkling clean. She zoomed up into the air to dry. Misty yellow trails appeared as she whooshed about. "That's better!" she cried.

She hovered in front of Kirsty. Her wings flashed like gold in the sun. Then she swooped onto Rachel's shoulder. "Come on, let's go to the pot-at-the-end-of-the-rainbow!"

Rachel nodded. She wanted to leave the garden before the goblins got there.

"Good-bye, Queenie!" Sunny called, waving to her friend.

Queenie looked out of the entrance to the hive. She seemed a bit sad that Sunny was going. Her feelers drooped as she waved a tiny leg and buzzed good-bye.

Sunny sat cross-legged on Rachel's shoulder as they headed for the woods. Suddenly, she cried out and flew up into the air. "Oh, no!" She gasped. "I left my wand beside the birdbath!"

Rachel looked at Kirsty in dismay. "We'll have to go back," she said.

"Yes," Kirsty agreed. "We can't leave a fairy wand lying around for the goblins to find."

"Oh, dear . . . Oh, dear . . ." Sunny zipped back and forth, wringing her hands as they went back along the path.

Rachel paused at the gate and looked into the garden. There was no sign of any goblins.

Kirsty and Rachel ran through the apple trees, straight to Queenie's hive. Sunny fluttered just above them.

Suddenly, an icy blast made them all
shiver. They gazed around in alarm.
Icicles now hung from the apple trees,
and the whole lawn was white and
crunchy with frost. The goblins had
arrived! And they'd brought winter to
the lovely yard.

Sunny gave a cry of horror.

An ugly, hook-nosed goblin jumped
up on top of Queenie's hive. His
bulging eyes gleamed, and in his hand
he was holding Sunny's wand!

Well Done, Queenie

"Give me back my wand!" Sunny demanded.

"Come and get it!" yelled the goblin rudely. He leaped off the hive and ran toward the gate.

Kirsty gasped as another goblin jumped down from the apple tree. *Splat!*

He landed on the frosty grass and set off at a run.

"Catch!" The goblin threw the wand to his friend. It flew through the air, shooting out yellow sparks.

The other goblin reached up and caught the wand. "Hee, hee. Got it!"

"Oh, no!" Sunny gasped.

Just then, Queenie flew out of the hive with a loud buzz. All the other bees swarmed behind her in a noisy cloud.

Rachel watched, her eyes very wide. With Queenie in the lead, the bees formed into an arrow shape and surged after the goblins.

"Be careful, Queenie!" pleaded
Sunny.

"Get away!" The goblin shook
Sunny's wand at Queenie.

More bright yellow sparks shot out
of the wand. One of the sparks hit
Queenie's wing. Queenie wobbled in
midair. Then she buzzed angrily and
flew at the goblin again.

"Help!" The goblin ducked and
dropped the wand.

"Butterfingers!" grumbled the other
goblin, scooping it up.

"They're getting
away!" Kirsty
said in dismay.

Queenie and her
bees rose into
the air again.

"No, they're
not!" Rachel cried
excitedly. The bees shot across the yard
and the goblins disappeared under an
angry, black cloud.

"Get off me!" spluttered the goblin
with the wand. He
tried to brush the
bees away, but
tripped over his
feet. As he fell,
he bumped into
the other goblin.

They tumbled over in a heap, dropping the wand onto the grass.

"That was your fault!" complained one of the goblins.

"No, it wasn't!" snapped the other one.

Queenie zoomed over and picked up the wand in her tiny, black feet.

She carried it straight to Sunny, who was standing on Rachel's hand. With a little buzz, Queenie landed next to Sunny.

Sunny took her wand from Queenie and carefully waved it in the air. A fountain of glittering dust and fluttering butterflies sparkled around them. "My wand is all right!" Sunny cried joyfully. "Look! The goblins are going," Kirsty said. The bees had chased the goblins to the edge of the yard. Still arguing, they ran across the fields.

As the grumbling voices faded away,
the icy wind dropped. The sun shone
warmly again and the frost melted. The
bees streamed back and flew around
Rachel and Kirsty, buzzing softly.

"Thank you, Queenie!" Sunny's eyes
sparkled as she hugged her friend.

Suddenly, Queenie wobbled and
tipped sideways.

Rachel cupped her hands, worried
that Queenie would roll off.
"I think she might
be hurt," she said.
Sunny knelt
down and
looked closely
at Queenie.
"Oh, no! She's torn
her wing!" She gasped.

"It must have happened when she fought the goblin," Rachel said.

"Can you mend Queenie's wing with magic?" Kirsty asked Sunny.

Sunny shook her head. "Not on my own. But Amber or Ruby might be able to help me. We have to take Queenie to the pot-at-the-end-of-the-rainbow right away!"

Fairy Repairs

Rachel and Kirsty hurried across the
fields and into the woods. Rachel
carefully held Queenie in her cupped
hands, while Sunny flew behind them,
her rainbow-colored wings shimmering
in the sun.

"There's the willow tree where the
pot is hidden," Kirsty said. She went

over and parted the branches, which
hung right down to the ground. The
black pot lay on its side in the grass. A
large, green frog hopped out from
behind it.

"Bertram!" Sunny flew down and
hugged him. "I'm so glad you're here!"

Bertram bowed his head. "It's a
pleasure, Miss Sunny,"
he said. "Miss Ruby
and Miss Amber
will be delighted
to see you."

Suddenly, a shower
of red and orange
fairy dust shot up out
of the pot, followed
by Ruby and Amber.

"Sunny!" Ruby shouted.
"It really is you!"
"It's good to have
you back," Amber
called happily.
Kirsty and Rachel
smiled as the fairies
hugged and kissed one another.

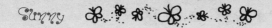

The air around them fizzed with red flowers, orange bubbles, and tiny, yellow butterflies.

Ruby flew onto Kirsty's shoulder. "Thank you, Rachel and Kirsty," she said. "Now three of us are safe." Then she spotted Queenie sitting on Rachel's hand. "Who is this?" she asked.

"This is my friend Queenie," Sunny explained. "She helped me get my wand back after the goblins stole it."

"Goblins?" Ruby shuddered. "You were very brave to fight them." She flew down and stroked Queenie's head.

"One of the goblins used my wand to hurt Queenie's wing. Can you help her?" Sunny asked her sisters.

Amber thought hard. "I could mend Queenie's wing if I had a fairy needle and thread," she said. Then she looked sad. "But I don't have any here on the island."

Then Rachel remembered something. "Kirsty! What about the magic bags that the Fairy Queen gave us?"

"Oh, yes," Kirsty said. She reached into her pocket and took out her bag. It was glowing with a soft, silver light. When she opened it, a cloud of glitter shot up into the air. Kirsty slipped her hand into the bag. "There's something here." She drew out a tiny, shining needle, threaded with fine

spider silk. She held it out to Amber. "Perfect!" Amber said. She flew onto Rachel's hand.

Sunny stroked Queenie's black-and-yellow head. "Don't worry," she said. "It's fairy magic, so it won't hurt."

Kirsty watched as Amber carefully wove the needle in and out of the tear. The row of stitches glowed like tiny silver dots.

"Look, they're starting to fade," Rachel said.

"Yes," said Amber. "When you can't see them anymore, the wing is mended."

Queenie buzzed softly. She lifted her head and flapped her wings. Then she  zoomed into the air. Her wing was as good as new! She swooped down and landed next to Amber. Bowing her head, she rubbed her feelers against the fairy's hand. "You have been such a good friend to Sunny, you have to stay with us," said Amber, hugging the bee. "Yes!" Ruby agreed. "Please come and live with us in the pot."

Queenie flew over to Sunny and buzzed in her ear.

"She says she would love to," said Sunny. "There is a hiveless queen in Mrs. Merry's yard who will take care of her bees. Come on, Queenie. Let's look at our new home."

"Let's take a look, too," Kirsty said. Rachel crouched down beside her in the grass. They watched the fairy sisters and the queen bee go into the pot.

Sunny beamed when she saw all the tiny furniture. She sat down on a soft, mossy cushion. "This is just like our home in Fairyland," she said. Then her face fell.

"But what about our sisters? They are
still trapped on the island!"

"Don't worry," Kirsty said. "We'll
find them soon."

"Yes, we will," Rachel agreed,
jumping up. She looked at her watch.
"It's nearly lunchtime. We have to go.
Good-bye, we'll see you again soon."

The fairies looked up and waved.
"Good-bye! Good-bye!" Queenie waved
a tiny leg and buzzed.

Bertram, the frog footman, followed them out from under the willow tree. "Ruby, Amber, and Sunny will be safe here with me," he said. "But you have to be careful when you go looking for the others. Watch out for goblins!"

"We will," Rachel promised.

Kirsty looked back at the pot-at-the-end-of-the-rainbow. "Nothing will stop us from finding the other Rainbow Fairies!" she said firmly.

RAINBOW
magic

Ruby, Amber, and Sunny are
out of danger. Now Rachel
and Kristy must free
Fern the Green Fairy

A Secret Garden

"Oh!" Rachel Walker gasped in
delight as she gazed around her.
"What a perfect place for a picnic!"

"It's a secret garden," Kirsty Tate
said, her eyes shining.

They were standing in a large
garden. It looked as if nobody else
had been there for a long, long time.

Pink and white roses grew all around
the tree trunks, filling the air with sweet
perfume. White marble statues stood
here and there, half hidden by trailing,
green ivy. And right in the middle of the
garden was a crumbling stone tower.

"There was a castle here once called
Moonspinner Castle," Mr. Walker said,
looking at his guidebook. "But now all
that's left is the tower."

Rachel and Kirsty stared up at the
ruined tower. The yellow stones glowed
warmly in the sunshine. They were
covered in soft, green moss. Near the top
of the tower was a small, square
window.

"It's just like Rapunzel's tower," Kirsty
said. "I wonder if we can get up to
the top."

"Let's go see!" Rachel said eagerly. "I want to explore the whole garden. Can we, Mom?"

"Go ahead." Mrs. Walker smiled. "Your dad and I will get the food ready." She opened the picnic basket. "But don't be too long, girls."

Rachel and Kirsty rushed over to the door in the side of the tower.

Read the rest of

RAINBOW
magic

Fern the Green Fairy
To find out what Rachel and Kirsty discover at the top of the tower.